I See You

Bus Stop

by Michael Genhart, PhD

illustrated by
Joanne Lew-Vriethoff

Magination Press • Washington, DC • American Psychological Association

To my parents, Ed & Rose Genhart, who first showed me what home means, and to John and Gabby, who make our home so wonderful today —*MG*

To Maarten with love—*JL-V*

Published by
MAGINATION PRESS®
An Educational Publishing Foundation Book
American Psychological Association
750 First Street NE
Washington, DC 20002

Magination Press is a registered trademark of the American Psychological Association.

For more information about our books, including a complete catalog, please write to us, call 1-800-374-2721, or visit our website at www.apa.org/pubs/magination.

Book design by Gwen Grafft
Printed by Worzalla, Stevens Point, WI

Library of Congress Cataloging-in-Publication Data
Names: Genhart, Michael, author. | Lew-Vriethoff, Joanne, illustrator.
Title: I see you / by Michael Genhart ; Illustrated by Joanne Lew-Vriethoff.
Description: Washington, DC : Magination Press, [2017] | "American
  Psychological Association." | Summary: "A wordless picture book that
  depicts a homeless woman who is not seen by all the life around her,
  except by a little boy. Ultimately, in a gesture of compassion, this boy
  approaches this woman, in an exchange where he sees her and she
  experiences being seen"— Provided by publisher. | Includes
  bibliographical references.
Identifiers: LCCN 2016050572| ISBN 9781433827587 (hardcover) |
  ISBN 1433827581 (hardcover)
Subjects: | CYAC: Homeless persons—Fiction. | Compassion—Fiction. |
  Stories without words.
Classification: LCC PZ7.1.G47 Iap 2017 | DDC [E]—dc23 LC record available
at https://lccn.loc.gov/2016050572

Manufactured in the United States of America
10 9 8 7 6 5 4 3 2 1

Note to Parents, Educators, and Neighbors

A wordless book might imply that there is not a lot to be said about a subject matter. This could not be further from the truth on the subject of homelessness. It's not uncommon for children, who lack our knowledge (and our biases), to be curious about the people they see living on the street. As an adult, it can be hard to know how to respond to these comments and questions. While people have different reactions to homelessness, the reality is that most of us simply ignore the problem. That is to say, for the most part we treat homeless people like they are invisible.

About Homelessness

Having a basic understanding of the problem ourselves is crucial when beginning a conversation with children. Homelessness, at its most basic level, happens when people are not able to acquire or maintain housing they can afford; it is where poverty and a lack of stable housing meet. It is important to remember that homelessness is a condition and not a label. Individuals are *experiencing* homelessness, often for complex reasons. The term "homeless," according to the US Department of Housing and Urban Development (HUD), pertains to someone who lives in an emergency shelter, transitional housing program (including safe havens), or a place not meant for human habitation, such as a car, abandoned building, or the streets. This also applies to anyone lacking appropriate housing after being evicted from a private dwelling unit, discharged from an institution (e.g. jail or mental health or substance abuse treatment facility), or fleeing a domestic violence situation. The National Alliance to End Homelessness (in America) estimates that there are between 550,000-650,000 people experiencing homelessness nationwide at any given time.

Depending on the age of your child, you might want to have a more detailed conversation about some of the causes of homelessness. It's important to note the wide variety of circumstances that can lead to a lack of adequate housing. Some people affected by homelessness may include: the working poor, people with disabilities, young adults who have recently been emancipated (or aged out) from the foster care system, and veterans struggling to adapt to civilian life (including finding sustainable work), among others. Some estimates suggest that around 8% of homeless people are unaccompanied youth and children (including up to one-third who are LGBTQ+ and have been kicked out of their homes). To fully understand homelessness, one must tackle several social issues, including: poverty; affordable housing; disabilities; (often untreated) mental illness, substance abuse, and addiction; the complicated needs of some veterans; and domestic violence, among others. The paucity of accessible and affordable housing in the United States, especially in urban areas where one sees more homelessness, is also key to the problem.

Some people are homeless for only a short while, often due to an unexpected catastrophic event or life change. Some people go in and out of homelessness, often because of medical issues, addiction issues, or mental illnesses, which can make it hard for them to maintain steady work and housing. And some people are chronically homeless, for any number of complex conditions.

Engendering Empathy

Children are naturally curious about everything, and sensitive subjects are no exception. As mentioned earlier, children are likely to have many questions about the homeless individuals they see and about homelessness in general. Some of these questions may be easy to answer factually, but for many, there may not be straight-forward answers. For questions like this, it can be helpful to have an honest and open conversation with your child about some of the problems our society faces and what they can do to help. The idea is to foster greater awareness and empathic conversations about homeless people *as people* in order to help see them in more humanitarian ways. Some questions children could have may include:

- How does homelessness happen? Who can become homeless?
- Where do they live? Where do they sleep?
- Where do they go to school?
- What do they eat?
- Where is their family?
- What should I say to a homeless person?
- Why do so many people ignore homeless people?
- How come some homeless people act in scary ways?
- Do their pets get proper care?
- What is it like for them living on the street?
- Why don't they go to a shelter?
- How can we help homeless people?

The experience of homelessness can happen to anyone depending on the circumstances that person is facing. When children ask questions, try to answer in a way that emphasizes the personhood of the individual. For instance, they may have a family somewhere, but that family may not be in a position to help them. Or they may not have a good relationship with their family. A child wondering why a homeless person has a pet can start a conversation about how that pet can offer important companionship just like they do for any other pet owner. After seeing homeless people living in a "tent city" or sleeping on the street, your child might ask, "Why don't they go to a shelter?" In this case, you could start a conversation where you note that sometimes they cannot bring belongings, pets, or partners to a shelter, or they simply feel their freedom or privacy is restricted in these places. Or your child might observe and comment on a person who is talking loudly to apparently no one, for example, which can be a time to gently explain that some people need help (e.g. psychological, emotional, substance-related) that they may not want or be able to find.

These are all hard questions with many possible answers, but the key is to have conversations using an empathetic tone. For younger children, answers should be direct but simple. With older children, you may be able to have a more in-depth discussion. For example, seeing homeless people sleeping in bus stops, doorways, or in front of public buildings might spark a conversation with an older child about the laws where you live. While it is not technically a crime to be homeless, in many cities around the world it is a crime to sleep in public spaces, to trespass, and to loiter and beg in public places, as well as to perform "life-sustaining" acts like using the bathroom. This issue illustrates how the rights and needs of different people collide: Where can these people without homes go? Do business owners and residents have the right to keep their premises clear of trespassers (sometimes by calling the police)? You could also start a conversation about how we as a society can offer people who are homeless a space for privacy and dignity (which is important for everyone).

Helping

Children are often vocal and uninhibited about their altruism; their reaction to learning about the issue of homelessness is very often to want to help. This is fantastic, and a quality that should be encouraged. However, the average adult often doesn't know the do's and don'ts of how best to proceed. Indeed, in some cases (e.g. homeless individuals with significant psychiatric issues or drug addiction), it can be quite challenging to know what can be done. And of course, children should never be encouraged to approach strangers, including anyone homeless, without the supervision of a responsible adult.

Giving

When discussing ways of giving with your child, perhaps first take into account things that are discouraged, such as: money, candy (since it's not healthy and can cause dental issues), your address, expensive items that may make them vulnerable to theft (including new clothing, with the exception of socks and underwear), and large cases of bakery items (since these items go stale quickly and often end up in the garbage). Alternatively, you might consider giving things like: new socks and underwear, hotel-size toiletries, clean (used) clothes and blankets, and bottles of water (unless your city or town prohibits this). Homeless individuals often know where in the community to get free meals, but many still appreciate the offer of a healthy meal or snack.

You might also engage your child in a conversation about how they appreciate being treated nicely, and emphasize that most homeless people probably feel the same way. As an alternative to giving "things" away to a homeless individual, try "hello," "good morning," or a simple nod instead of looking the other way. You can learn their names, listen, and remember them. These are acts of acknowledgment, kindness, and respect, and a way to treat someone as human and not invisible. Some people offer a homeless individual a prayer or a wish of good will—a kind of hope that they might really need.

Getting Involved

Parents can decide together with their children how they may want to do more to help. For example, as a family, you might volunteer in some capacity at a shelter, at an organization that cooks and feeds hot meals to people, at a local food bank, with a non-profit group that delivers meals to individuals, or by contributing time to an organization that collects and distributes clothing and hygienic supplies.

The **National Coalition for the Homeless** lists some great ideas about how anyone might want to get involved in helping people who are experiencing homelessness. Other organizations such as **justgive.org** have developed similar lists to assist people in thinking about different ways they can help out. These efforts focus on reducing stereotyping and stigmatization as well as offering practical advice on how to volunteer. The next page lists some more organizations that emphasize combating homelessness as a humanitarian effort and are always looking for help.

Do at Home: Care Bags!

Many people are unsure how to respond if a homeless person approaches them for help; they generally don't have food on them, and are uncomfortable giving out money. One young woman and her mother did research into the best things to give out, and came up with these little Care Bags. You can vary yours, but the idea is to keep them small so that you can have some on hand most places you go.

Good things to include:

- small non-perishable foods (sealed packets of applesauce, beef jerky, crackers, etc.)
- wet wipes
- travel-sized toothbrushes & toothpaste tubes
- feminine care products

Some things to avoid:

- hard foods & candy
- things containing alcohol, like mouthwash & hand sanitizer

National Alliance to End Homelessness. This group is a leading voice on the issue of homelessness. They analyze policy and develop effective policy solutions in collaboration with public, private, and non-profit programs with the aim of ending homelessness.

National Coalition for Homeless Veterans. The goal of the NCHV is to end homelessness among veterans by shaping public policy, promoting collaboration, and building the capacity of service providers.

StandUp for Kids. Their mission is to end the cycle of youth homelessness.

Adopt a Family (of your local area). The core mission of this group is to prevent homelessness by providing stability for families in need.

Homeward Bound (of your local area). Homeward Bound provides homeless shelters and services for homeless families and individuals.

Operation Warm Wishes. This organization is dedicated to helping and serving homeless troubled youth, struggling families, veterans, and senior citizens.

Miracle Messages. This is an organization that aims to reconnect homeless people with their loved ones through videos and social media.

Project Night Night. This organization donates packages consisting of a security blanket, an age-appropriate children's book, and a stuffed animal to homeless children below age 12.

Pets of the Homeless. This is an organization which supports (through collecting pet food and pet supplies) the healing power of companion pets and the human-animal bond, especially in the lives of homeless individuals.

About the Author

Michael Genhart, PhD is a licensed clinical psychologist in private practice in San Francisco and Mill Valley, California. He lives with his family in Marin County. He received his BA in psychology from the University of California, San Diego and his PhD in clinical and community psychology from the University of Maryland, College Park. He is the author of several picture books including: *Ouch! Moments: When Words Are Used in Hurtful Ways* (2016), *So Many Smarts!* (2017), *Mac & Geeez!* (2017), *Cake & I Scream!* (2017), and *Peanut Butter & Jellyous* (2017), all from Magination Press, as well as *Yes We Are!* (Little Pickle Press/Sourcebooks, 2018).

About the Illustrator

Joanne Lew-Vriethoff is a talented artist whose passion and love for storytelling is shown through her whimsical but heartfelt illustrations in picture and chapter books in both the Dutch and English language. Joanne lives with her gorgeous husband and two wild, sensitive children, a girl and a boy. Together they discover the world by traveling, collecting memories and deriving inspiration for her art along the way. She currently lives in Amsterdam with her family.

About Magination Press

Magination Press is an imprint of the American Psychological Association, the largest scientific and professional organization representing psychologists in the United States and the largest association of psychologists worldwide.